HELLO KITTY'S PAPER KISS

by Sarah Bright • illustrated by Bruce McGowin

RANDOM HOUSE 🏠 NEW YORK

Copyright © 1982 by Sanrio Co. Ltd. All rights reserved under International and Pan-American Copyright Conventions. Published in the United States by Random House, Inc., New York, and simultaneously in Canada by Random House of Canada Limited, Toronto. *Library of Congress Cataloging in Publication Data:* Bright, Sarah. Hello Kitty's paper kiss. SUMMARY: A little girl misses her father when he goes on a trip. [1. Fathers and daughters—Fiction] I. McGowin, Bruce. II. Title. PZ7.B7652Hf [E] AACR2 82-3734 ISBN: 0-394-85398-9 Manufactured in the United States of America
1 2 3 4 5 6 7 8 9 0

Daddy was going on a trip. Kitty watched him pack his bag. She felt a little sad.

"I'll be back on Friday," Daddy said.

He kissed Mama and Kitty good-bye. Mama and Kitty waved to him.

"Come back soon," said Kitty. Daddy blew them a kiss.

That night Mama cooked Kitty's favorite dinner.

"I'm not hungry," said Kitty.

Daddy's chair looked very empty.

"Friday will be here soon," said Mama.

Mama let Kitty stay up and play after her bath.

When the phone rang, she let Kitty answer it.

It was Daddy! "I'll see you on Friday," he said. He sent Kitty a kiss. It went right into her ear.

At bedtime Mama read Kitty two stories.

"I miss having a Daddy hug," said Kitty.

Mama gave her a Mama hug and sang a sleepy song.

Not the next day, but the day after that, the mailman brought a letter for Kitty.

In the letter Daddy wrote: "Here is a paper kiss and a paper hug for you." He had drawn a big red X and a big green O.

"Let's put them on the refrigerator," said Kitty.

Kitty loved to look at her letter.

The next morning, when Kitty woke up, she asked, "Is today Friday?"

"Today is Thursday," said Mama. "Tomorrow is Friday."

That night at bedtime Kitty felt sad. She missed Daddy. "Tonight you can sleep in Daddy's bed," said Mama.

When Kitty woke up, Mama said, "Today is Friday. We will cook a special dinner for Daddy."

"I will make chocolate pudding," said Kitty.

When Daddy came home, he gave Kitty a real kiss and a real hug.

"Now we can take the paper kiss and hug off the refrigerator," said Kitty.

So Daddy lifted her up, and she did.